KT-466-426

This book belongs to

_____

_____

Aged _____

Wake up Muffin

AND OTHER STORIES

Wake up Muffin

AND OTHER STORIES

p

This is a Parragon Book
This edition published in 2002

Parragon
Queen Street House
4 Queen Street
Bath BA1 1HE, UK

Copyright © Parragon 2000

ISBN 0-75258–423-5

Designed by Mik Martin

Printed in Italy

These stories have been previously
published by Parragon in the
Bumper Bedtime Series

CONTENTS

Wake Up, Muffin

CATS LOOK so comfortable when they are asleep. Somehow they always manage to find the warmest, cosiest spot in the whole house. And often it's the very spot where you most want to sit yourself!

But some cats seem to want to sleep most of the time, and that can be particularly annoying if what you'd really like to do is to play with them.

Helena had a cat called Muffin. The little girl loved him very much. She couldn't remember him when he was a kitten, because she was only a baby herself then, but even now, Muffin wasn't an old cat. He was only four, just like Helena.

But Helena was a lively little girl, and Muffin was a very sleepy cat. Very often, when Helena wanted Muffin to join in one of her games, he was fast asleep on the sofa.

"Wake up, Muffin!" Helena would call, bending close to one of the cat's furry little ears.

Muffin's ear would twitch, just a little bit.

"Wake up, Muffin!" Helena would shout, louder this time, bending a little closer.

Muffin's ear would twitch a little bit more. Helena would take a deep breath and lean forward until she was almost touching the soundly sleeping cat.

"Wake up, Muffin!" she would yell, so loudly that her mother could hear her from the kitchen.

And Muffin? He would open one lazy eye. He would twitch his whiskers and have a little stretch. And he would go right back to sleep again.

It was so annoying! Helena tried being extra specially nice to Muffin. She stroked his fur gently and tickled his fat tummy. She sang him little songs about mice and kittens. But nothing worked. Muffin would simply purr with pleasure and stay fast asleep.

One day, Helena badly wanted Muffin to play with her. She was tired of her dolls, who were nothing

like as warm and cuddly as her cat.
She put her doll in its pram and
tucked a quilt round it.

"You just go to sleep like a good
girl, Hettie-Marie," she said (for that
was the doll's name).

Helena searched everywhere for
Muffin. He wasn't on the sofa, which
was his favourite place. He wasn't
under the table or next to the
radiator. At last she found him fast
asleep (of course!) on the quilt of
her parents' bed.

As she looked down at the
sleeping cat, Helena had a brilliant
idea.

She bent down and gently put
her arms around Muffin. He wasn't

Jimbo
Comes
Home

JIMBO the circus elephant was snoring away in his cage one night when he heard a strange noise. At first he thought it was part of his dream. In his dream he was walking across a hot, dusty plain while in the distance there was the sound of thunder.

All at once Jimbo was wide awake. He realised that he was in his cage after all and that what he thought was the sound of thunder was the noise of his cage on the move. Now this worried him, because the circus never moved at night. He rose to his feet and looked around. He could see men pulling on the tow bar at the front of the cage. These were strangers — it certainly wasn't Carlos his trainer! Jimbo started to bellow, "Help! Stop thief!" But it was too late. His cage was already rumbling out of the circus ground and down the road.

Eventually, the cage passed through a gate marked 'Zipper's

Circus' and Jimbo knew what had happened. He had been stolen by the Zipper family, his own circus family's greatest rivals! Jimbo was furious. How had the thieves got away with it? Surely someone at Ronaldo's Circus must have heard them stealing him? But Jimbo waited in vain to be rescued.

The next morning, the thieves opened up Jimbo's cage and tried to coax him out, but he stayed put. In the end, after much struggling, they managed to pull him out. Once he was out of his cage, he took the biggest drink of water he could from a bucket and soaked his new keeper! He refused to cooperate, kicked over his food, and when he appeared in the circus that night he made sure he got all the tricks wrong.

"Don't worry," said Mr Zipper to Jimbo's new trainer, "he'll just take a little while to settle down. Soon he'll forget that he was once part of Ronaldo's Circus." But Jimbo didn't forget for, as you know, an elephant never forgets.

The other animals in Zipper's Circus had all been stolen from other circuses, too. "You'll just have to get used to it here," said one of the chimps to Jimbo. "It's not so bad really." But Jimbo decided he was going to try and escape.

One night, a mouse passed by his cage. "Hello," called Jimbo mournfully, for by now he was feeling very lonely, and no-one had cleaned his cage out for days.

"Hello!" said the mouse. "You don't look very happy. What's the matter?" Jimbo explained how he had been stolen and wanted to escape back to his own circus.

The mouse listened and then said, "I'll try to help." So saying, he scampered off and soon he was back with a bunch of keys. Jimbo was astonished.

"Easy!" said the mouse. "The keeper was asleep, so I helped myself."

Jimbo took the keys in his trunk and unlocked the door to the cage. He was free! "Thank you!" he called to the mouse, who was already scurrying away.

Jimbo's first thought was to get back to his own circus as fast as possible. However, he wanted to teach those thieves a lesson. He could hear them snoring in their caravan. He tiptoed up, as quietly as an elephant can tiptoe, and slid into the horse's harness at the front. "Hey, what do you think you're doing?" neighed one of the horses, but Jimbo was already hauling the robbers' caravan out of the gate and down the road.

So gently did he pull the caravan
that the thieves never once woke
up. Eventually they reached
Ronaldo's Circus. Mr Ronaldo was
dumbstruck to see Jimbo pulling a
caravan just like a horse! Mr Ronaldo
walked over to the caravan and was

astonished to see the robbers still fast asleep. He raced to the telephone and called the police, and it wasn't until they heard the police siren that the robbers woke up. By then it was too late. As they emerged from the caravan scratching and shaking their heads they were arrested on the spot and taken off to jail.

"There are a few questions we would like to ask Mr Zipper regarding the theft of some other circus animals, too," said one of the police officers.

Mr Ronaldo, and Jimbo's keeper Carlos, were both delighted to see Jimbo back home again. And Jimbo was just as delighted to be back home. Then Mr Ronaldo and Carlos started whispering to each other and began walking away looking secretive. "We'll be back soon, we promise," they said to Jimbo. When they returned, they were pushing Jimbo's old cage. It had been freshly painted, there was clean, sweet-smelling straw inside, but best of all there was no lock on the door!

"Now you can come and go as you please," said Carlos.

And Jimbo trumpeted long and loud with his trunk held high, which Carlos knew was his way of saying, "THANK YOU!"

Maurice the Minnow's Dangerous Journey

MAURICE THE MINNOW lived in a beautiful, reed-fringed pond in a clearing in the middle of a small woodland. He had been born one fine spring morning, and now he spent each day swimming happily in the shallows with all his little minnow brothers and sisters.

But life in the pond had its dangers, too! He had heard alarming stories about a kingfisher that would dive into the water from a branch overhanging the pond and grab tiny fish and swallow them down. And then there was the heron — a great, grey, stalking bird that suddenly loomed into the shallows and snatched unsuspecting fish with its great beak.

But the stories Maurice feared most were the ones about Lucius the pike. Lucius had lived in the pond for longer than anyone could remember. Woe betide you if you met Lucius when he was hungry, for he would dart out from his hiding place among the water weeds, and you would be gone! Nothing ever escaped from his huge jaws, which were lined with needle-sharp teeth. Maurice had heard tales of Lucius swallowing fish bigger than Maurice could imagine — not to mention ducks, voles and other animals of the

pond. Why, there was even a rumour that Lucius had once snatched a dog from the bank and taken it down to the depths of the pond to devour it!

Maurice's mother had said that the best way to avoid meeting Lucius was to always stay in the shallows, and never swim across the pond, for it was in the deep, dark waters that Lucius loved to hunt.

One sunny summer's day, Maurice and his brothers and sisters were swimming in the shallows as usual, when suddenly he felt himself being lifted up and out of the water. The next thing he knew he was flapping helplessly in the bottom of a net, gasping for breath. Mercifully, he soon found himself back in the water again, but it seemed different now. It was light all around and there were no welcoming, sheltering weeds to hide in. And where were all his brothers and sisters? Next, to his horror, he saw a huge, unfamiliar creature staring at him. He'd heard no stories about anything as big as this! The creature's head seemed so close that Maurice felt certain he was about to be eaten. But just as suddenly the creature seemed to move away, and Maurice felt himself being carried along in this new, strange, watery world.

Maurice was wondering if he was to be trapped in this new, small pond forever when just as suddenly as he seemed to have entered the pond, he was now leaving it again. He felt himself falling down, down, until — with a splash — he was

back in his own pond again. Or at least, it seemed like his pond, but nothing was quite as familiar as it had been. Finding a clump of water weed, he immediately dived under it for safety, while he considered

"Hello, you're new here, aren't you?" a friendly voice said. Maurice looked round in surprise to find himself face to face with a frog. He told the frog about his horrible adventure while the frog listened patiently, nodding wisely from time to time.

"Well, we know what's happened to you, don't we?" said the frog when Maurice had finished. "You got caught in a little boy's fishing net. They're often about around here. I've no doubt the big creature you saw was just the little boy looking at you swimming in his jam jar full of water. And now he's decided to put you back. The only trouble is, you're far from home. You live on the other side of the pond. And to get you back means we have got to go on a very dangerous journey."

Maurice didn't like the sound of this at all, but he missed his family terribly and knew that he would never be able to get back home without the kind frog's help. So without more ado, the two of them set off for their journey across the deep, dark pond.

"Swim near the surface. It's safer," advised the frog, "but keep a close eye out for kingfishers."

They seemed to have been swimming for ages, when suddenly a great, dark shadow appeared beneath them.

"It's Lucius!" cried the frog in fright.

Before either of them could escape, they found themselves face to face with the dreaded pike.

"Well, well," leered Lucius. "I can't believe my luck! A frog *and* a minnow. Lunch and supper together if I'm not mistaken!"

So saying, he opened his enormous jaws and was about to swallow them whole when — BOINK! — a huge, flat stone landed right on Lucius's head. Dazed, Lucius sank slowly towards the bottom of the pond.

"Quick! It's our chance to escape!" yelled the frog. The two friends swam for their lives. Maurice kept thinking that any moment Lucius would reappear, but he needn't have worried. Lucius had too big a headache to think about hunting for a while yet!

Then suddenly Maurice was home. He recognised his own little part of the pond, and there swimming in the shallows was his family.

"I can't thank you enough," said Maurice gratefully to the frog. "But what *did* happen to Lucius?"

"You can thank the little boy who caught you in the net for our

escape," said the frog. "He was skimming stones across the pond and luckily Lucius's head got in the way!"

Maurice decided that he'd had quite enough adventures for one day, and found himself a cosy piece of water weed to hide under. Soon he was fast asleep.

Mr Mole
Gets Lost

MR MOLE poked his little black nose out from the top of one of his mole hills and gave a great big sniff of the air. Then he sniffed again. And then a third time just to make sure. "Oh dear," he thought, "it smells like it's going to rain."

Mr Mole didn't like the rain one bit. Every time he got caught in the rain his plush little velvet fur coat got all wet and drippy, and he left muddy footprints all over his underground burrow. But worse still, the rain got in through the holes in his mole hills and then everything got all soggy and took days to dry out.

Well, the skies got darker and darker, and very soon little spots of rain began to fall. Then the spots became bigger. And then bigger still. Before long, all you could see before your eyes were big, straight rods of rain bouncing off the leaves on the trees, pounding the ground and turning everything muddy and wet.

Mr Mole had never seen rain like it. He sat in his burrow in the middle of the meadow wishing it would stop. But it just kept raining and raining. Soon the rain started entering his burrow. First it went drip, drip, drip through the holes in his mole hills, and then it became a little river of water in the bottom of his burrow. Then the little river became a bigger, faster-flowing river and suddenly Mr Mole was being washed along by it. Through the tunnels of his burrow he went, this way and then that, as the water gushed and poured through his underground home.

The next thing he knew he was being washed out of his burrow completely as the rain water carried him off down the meadow. Down he went, not knowing which way up he was or where he was going. Now he was being washed through the woods at the bottom of the meadow, but still the water carried him on, bouncing and turning him until he was dizzy and gasping for breath.

Suddenly, he came to a halt. The rain water gurgled and trickled around him and then flowed onwards, as he found himself stuck firmly in the branches of a bush. "Oh dear," Mr Mole said as he got himself free. "Goodness me, where

can I be?" he thought. Mr Mole
looked around him, but being a
very short-sighted mole — as most
moles are — he couldn't make out
any of the places that were familiar
to him. Worse still, he couldn't
smell any smells that were familiar

to him. He was completely lost, far from home, and had no idea how to get back again. Now, to make things worse, it was starting to get dark.

"Woo-oo-oo-oo-oo!" said a voice suddenly. Mr Mole nearly jumped out of his moleskin with fright. "I wouldn't stay here if I were you," said the voice again. Mr Mole looked up and found himself face to face with an enormous owl. "Don't you know it's not safe in the woods at night?" asked the owl. "There are snakes and foxes and weasels and all sorts of nasty creatures that you really wouldn't like to meet."

"Oh dear!" was all Mr Mole could think of saying. He told the owl of his terrible watery journey and how he was lost and didn't know how to get back home again.

"You need to talk to Polly Pigeon," said the owl. "She is a homing pigeon and she lives near your meadow. She can show you the way home. But we'll have to find her first. Stay close to me, mind, and look out for those snakes, foxes and weasels I told you about."

Mr Mole didn't need telling twice. He stayed so close to the kindly owl that every time the owl stopped or turned round to talk to Mr Mole, Mr Mole bumped right into him!

Through the dark, dangerous woods they went. Every now and again, there would be an unfriendly noise, such as a deep growl or a hiss, coming from the dense,

tangled trees, but Mr Mole didn't want to think about that too much, so he just made sure that he never lost sight of the owl.

Finally, just when Mr Mole thought that he couldn't go a step further, they came to a halt by an old elm tree.

"Hallo-oooo," called the owl.

They were in luck. Polly Pigeon was waking up, and they found her just in time for she was about to continue her journey home.

"Please," said Mr Mole, "I'm afraid I'm terribly lost and don't know how to get back to my meadow. Will you take me there?"

"Of course I will," said Polly Pigeon. "We'd better let you rest here a while first, though. But we must go before it gets light."

So Mr Mole was soon trudging wearily back to his meadow, following as closely behind Polly Pigeon as he was able. Just as the first rays of sun lit the morning sky, Mr Mole smelled a very familiar smell. It was his meadow! He was almost home!

Soon, he was back in his own burrow. It was so wet and muddy, however, that the first thing he did was build some new tunnels higher up the meadow so that the rain wouldn't wash down into them so easily. Then he settled down to eat one of his supplies of worms, and fell into a deep, well-earned slumber.

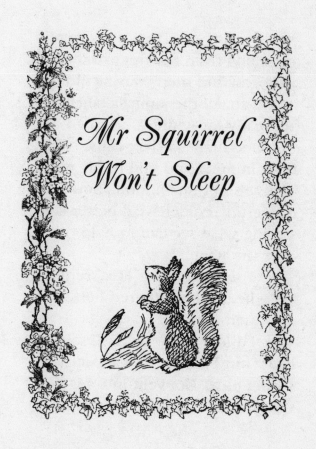

Mr Squirrel Won't Sleep

IT WAS AUTUMN. The leaves were falling from the trees in the forest and there was a cold nip in the air. All the animals began to get ready for winter.

One night Mr Fox came back from hunting and said to his wife, "There's not much food about now it's getting colder. We'd better start storing what we can to help tide us over the winter."

"You're right, Mr Fox," replied his wife, as she gathered her cubs into their lair.

"I'd love to go fishing," said Mr Bear, "but I'll have to wait until spring now." He went into his den, shut the door tight and sealed it.

"Well, I'm off for a holiday in the sun," announced Mrs Cuckoo, preening her feathers. "See you all next year!" she called as she took to the wing and flew south.

Mrs Mouse ran by with a mouthful of straw. "Must dash," she squeaked, "or my winter bed will

never be finished in time." But soon she, too, was curled up with her tail wrapped around her for warmth.

Now only Mr Squirrel wasn't ready for winter. He danced about in his tree, leaping from branch to branch and chasing his tail. "Ha, ha!" he boasted. "I don't have to get ready for winter. I have a fine store of nuts hidden away, a beautiful bushy tail to keep me warm and besides, I don't feel in the least bit sleepy." And he carried on playing in his tree.

"Are you still awake?" snapped Mr Fox.

"Go to sleep!" growled Mr Bear.

"Please be quiet," squeaked Mrs

Mouse, drawing her tail more tightly about her ears.

But Mr Squirrel wouldn't go to sleep. Not a bit of it. He danced up and down all the more and shouted, "I'm having SUCH FUN!" at the top of his voice.

Winter came. The wind whistled in the trees' bare branches, the sky turned grey and it became bitterly cold.

Then it started to snow. At first Mr Squirrel had a grand time making snowballs — but there was no-one around to throw them at and he began to feel rather lonely. Soon he felt cold and hungry, too.

"No problem!" he said to

himself. "I'll have some nice nuts to eat. Now, where did I bury them?" He scampered down his tree to find that the ground was deep with snow. He ran this way and that trying to find his hiding places, but all the forest looked the same in the snow and soon he was hopelessly lost.

"Whatever shall I do?" he whimpered, for now he was shivering with cold and hunger and his beautiful, bushy.tail was all wet and bedraggled.

All of a sudden he thought he heard a small voice. But where was it coming from? He looked all around but there was no sign of anyone. Then he realised that the voice was coming from under the snow. "Hurry up!" said the voice. "You can join me down here, but you'll have to dig a path to my door."

Mr Squirrel started digging frantically with his front paws and sure enough there was a path leading to a door under a tree stump. The door was slightly open — open enough for Mr Squirrel to squeeze his thin, tired body through.

Inside was a warm, cosy room with a roaring fire, and sitting by the fire was a tiny elf. "I heard you running around up there and thought you might be in need of a bit of shelter," said the elf. "Come and warm yourself by the fire." Mr Squirrel was only too pleased to accept and soon he was feeling warm and dry.

"This isn't my house, you know," said the elf. "I think it might be part of an old badgers' sett. I got lost in the forest and so when I

found this place, I decided to stay here until spring. Though how I'll ever find my way home, I don't know." A fat tear rolled down the elf's cheek.

"I have been a very foolish squirrel," said Mr Squirrel. "If you hadn't taken me in I surely would

have died. I am indebted to you and if you will let me stay here until spring, I will help you find your way home."

"Of course you can stay," replied the elf. "I'd be glad of the company." So Mr Squirrel settled down with his tail for a blanket and soon he was fast asleep.

Days and nights passed, until one day the elf popped his head out of the door and exclaimed, "The snow has melted, spring is coming. Wake up, Mr Squirrel." Mr Squirrel rubbed his eyes and looked out. It was true. There were patches of blue in the sky and he could hear a bird singing.

"Climb upon my back," Mr Squirrel said to the elf. "I'm going to show you the world." They set off through the forest until they came to the highest tree of all.

"Hold tight!" called Mr Squirrel as he climbed up through the branches until finally they reached the very top of the tree.

"You can look now," said Mr Squirrel, seeing that the elf had put his tiny hands over his eyes. The elf uncovered his eyes and stared and stared. He had never seen anything like it in his whole life. Stretching in all directions, as far as the eye could see, were mountains, lakes, rivers, forests and fields.

"What's that silvery-blue thing in the distance?" asked the elf.

"Why, that's the sea!" replied Mr Squirrel.

Suddenly the elf started to jump for joy.

"What is it?" said Mr Squirrel.

"I… I… can see my home," cried the elf, pointing down into the valley below the forest. "And there's my wife sitting in a chair in the sunshine. I must go home, Mr Squirrel. Thank you for showing me the world, for I should never have seen my home again without you." And with that he climbed down the tree and skipped all the way home.

Mr Squirrel made his way back to his own tree.

"Where have you been?" said Mr Fox.

"We've been looking for you," said Mr Bear.

"I'm glad you're home," said Mrs Mouse.

"So am I," said Mr Squirrel. "I've been very foolish, but I've learned my lesson. Now let's have a party — I've got rather a lot of nuts that need eating up!"

So the animals celebrated spring with a fine feast. And Mr Squirrel vowed not to be silly again next winter.

Good Neighbours

RUDDINGTON BUNNY lived a quiet life. Every morning, after breakfast, he tidied his house. Then he read the newspaper. Sometimes he played chess with his friend Ashby Squirrel. In the afternoon, he did his shopping. And in the evening, there was nothing Ruddington liked better than a cup of blackberry tea by the fire, and a good book to read.

Ruddington enjoyed his life. Everything about it seemed absolutely perfect — until the day Scarrington Owl moved into the house just above Ruddington's.

Oh, Scarrington was friendly enough. And he was kind and

generous and kept his house tidy. He was a good neighbour. In fact, thought Ruddington, Scarrington Owl would have been a perfect neighbour if it hadn't been for one thing.

Scarrington was noisy!

Every night, just about the time Ruddington was getting ready for bed, Scarrington Owl was just waking up. And when Ruddington was snuggled down under the covers, all set to drift off to dreamland, Scarrington began to hoot.

"Hoo-hoo-hooooo," Scarrington hooted. "Hoo-hoo-HOOOOO! Hoo-hoo-HOOOOOO-hoooo-hoo!" On and on it went, all through the night. Poor Ruddington tossed and turned and just couldn't get any sleep at all.

"I'll have to do something," Ruddington muttered one night. Wearily, he stumbled out of bed and went to the window.

"Please keep your voice down," he shouted out of the open window.

But Scarrington was hooting so loudly, he didn't hear.

In desperation, Ruddington went to his broom cupboard and got out his long-handled mop. Ruddington banged the mop handle hard against the ceiling. BANG! BANG! BANG! Scarrington hooted even louder.

"I'll have to go up there myself," muttered Ruddington, putting on his dressing gown as quickly as he could.

So upstairs Ruddington Bunny climbed, and he knocked on Scarrington's door.

"Excuse me," he said, when Scarrington answered his knock, "but it's two in the morning, and I'm trying to get to sleep. Do you think you could hoot just a little less loudly?"

"Oh dear," said Scarrington. "I'm ever so sorry for the disturbance. I'll try to keep the noise down."

"Thank you," said Ruddington, stumbling back downstairs. He was so tired that he was almost asleep before he got back into his bed.

For the next two nights, Scarrington's hooting was a bit softer, and Ruddington thought his sleepless nights were a thing of the past. But on the third night, the hooting got louder, and on the fourth night, it was louder still. By the end of the week, things were just as bad as they ever were.

"I'm sorry," said Scarrington, when Ruddington came to see him again. "Owls just have to hoot at night. It's what we do, and the louder we can do it, the better. I'm afraid you'll just have to put up with it. After all, we are neighbours, and neighbours have to

learn to live with one another, don't they?"

When Ashby came to visit the next morning, Ruddington said, "I'm sorry, but I'm just too tired to play chess today."

"Is it your noisy neighbour again?" asked Ashby looking sympathetically at his friend.

"Yes," wailed Ruddington. "I don't know what to do!"

"Why not try wearing earmuffs to bed?" suggested Ashby. "That's what I did when the moles who live downstairs from me had triplets. The babies cried and cried every night, but I never heard a thing."

It was worth a try, thought Ruddington. So that afternoon he went out and bought a pair of thick, fluffy earmuffs.

But a bunny needs very big earmuffs, and they made poor

Ruddington terribly hot and uncomfortable. In the end, he had to take them off.

One day, Ruddington's cousin Bingham Bunny came to visit.

"I once lived next door to a family of very rowdy hedgehogs," said Bingham. "I put pillows on my walls, and that muffled the noise. Maybe that would work for you, too."

So that evening, Ruddington taped some pillows to his ceiling. Bingham was right — it did muffle the noise, and Ruddington fell into a deep, contented sleep.

But in the middle of the night, the pillows fell down.

Ruddington woke with a start

— and a whole mouthful of feathers!

"It's no use," Ruddington said to himself the next morning. "I will just have to move house. It's the only way I will ever have any peace and quiet again."

Ruddington was all set to go out and see if there were any houses for rent, and had started to think about just what kind of home he would be looking for, when the post came through the door. Among the circulars and the bills, there was a very fancy envelope addressed to him, and when he opened it, he was certainly most surprised.

The card inside said:

You are invited to
a musical evening presented by

**THE OWL OPERATIC
SOCIETY**

at the home of
Scarrington Owl

7:00 PM tonight Refreshments will be served

So, at seven o'clock precisely,
Ruddington Bunny climbed the
stairs to Scarrington's house. He
was pleased to see that Ashby and
Cousin Bingham were both there,

as well as lots of other friends and neighbours. And all the owls of the forest were there, dressed in their very best outfits. There was a long table, spread with delicious things to eat and drink, and everyone seemed in a festive mood.

After a few minutes, Scarrington cleared his throat. "Ladies and gentlemen," he announced. "Please be seated. Our recital is about to begin."

Everyone sat down, and the owls gathered together at the front of the room, standing very smartly in rows.

"Hoo-hoo-hoo-hooo," sang Scarrington, to give the others the key — and the singing began.

It was magnificent! All hooting in harmony, the owls sang their way through dozens of wonderful songs. They sang slow, romantic, sentimental songs, and quick, bright, funny songs. They even sang loud songs and soft ones, happy songs and sad ones. They even took requests and sang special favourites — and everyone joined in the choruses. As the moon rose, and stars twinkled in sky, the music of happy voices filled the forest.

Much later, as dawn broke, the singing finally came to an end, and everyone prepared to fly, scamper, shuffle and hop home. Before he left, Ruddington went up to Scarrington.

"Thank you so much for inviting me," he said. "I can't remember when I've had so much fun! And now that I know how delightful your hooting can be, I'm sure it won't bother me any more."

"I'm glad you had a good time," said Scarrington. "And I have some special news for you."

"Oh?" said Ruddington.

"Yes," said Scarrington Owl. "There's no need for you to worry about the noise any longer. The Owl Operatic Society has found a splendid new rehearsal hall. Starting tomorrow, you'll be glad to know that we'll be practising our hooting and singing in our very own tree."

"But you're not moving away?" asked Ruddington, anxiously.

"Of course not!" exclaimed Scarrington. "This tree will always be my home."

"Oh, I'm glad," said Ruddington Bunny. "Because, you know, you've become much more than a neighbour — you're also a very special friend!"

The
Real
Baby
Doll

ONE DAY, Beatrice's mother gave her a present. This was strange, because it wasn't Christmas, or her birthday, or a special day of any kind. Inside the wrapping paper was a baby doll, wearing a little white stretchy suit and with its own shawl and bottle of milk.

"I don't like dolls," said Beatrice. "And I specially don't like baby dolls. They don't do anything."

Beatrice's mother sighed. "Well, no, they don't do anything much at first," she said, "except sleep and drink their milk, but they need you to do something. They need you to love them and look after them. I think you could do that, Bea, couldn't you?"

"Why should I?" asked Beatrice. "I like toys that move or play tunes or light up or something. Not like this silly doll."

The little girl's mother tried again. "The reason I thought you might like a baby doll to look after," she said, "is that I'm going to be having a baby soon — a little sister for you, Bea — and I thought it would be fun if we could both look after our babies together."

But Beatrice looked at her Mum with a big scowl on her face. "You can take this doll back," she said, "and you can take your baby back, too. We're quite happy as we are, aren't we? We don't need one of those silly babies here. Don't let's talk about it any more. Promise?"

"I can't take either of the babies back, Bea," said her mother gently. "Perhaps you'll change your mind in a little while."

But Beatrice continued to show no interest at all in the baby doll. Her mother showed her how to wash it and feed it and cuddle it. But Bea was always impatient to get back to her other toys. She hid the doll in a cupboard, but somehow her mother always found it and brought it out again.

A few weeks later, Beatrice's

father came into her room late one night. "Aunty Julia has come to look after you tonight, Bea," he said, "because I'm going with Mummy to get our new baby. Isn't it exciting?"

"Well, I hope you're not going to bring it back here," said Beatrice. "I told Mummy we don't need it."

But in the morning, Daddy came back and carried Beatrice into the sitting room. Mummy was propped up on the sofa, and in her arms she held a little pink and white bundle.

"Come and see our baby, Bea," she said, and she looked rather anxiously at her little girl.

Beatrice came forward and put

out her hand. She touched the baby's soft little hand and cried out in amazement. "But she's warm! She's not like a doll at all!"

And the baby, hearing her sister's voice, closed her little fingers around Beatrice's thumb.

"Oh, Mum," breathed Beatrice, "I've got such a good idea. You can have my baby doll, and I'll have this one. She's much, much nicer." And she bent down to kiss the little head.

"Let's share her," said her mother. "This little one belongs to all of us."

Della Duck's Adventure

WHEN AMY was a baby, her big brother gave her a yellow duck to play with in her bath. Amy loved playing with it from the start. She tried to drown it every night, but the little duck always came bobbing up to the surface again, as large as life.

A few weeks later, Amy tried to get rid of the duck in another way.

Over and over again, she threw it as far as she could with her chubby little arms. She got so good at throwing that the duck often hit the bathroom wall and bounced back again, sometimes falling with a *plop!* right back into the bath. Night after night, Amy's mother, or her father, or her big brother patiently picked up the duck and put it back in the water.

As Amy got bigger, the duck had lots more attacks to suffer. One summer's day, Amy threw it right out of the bathroom window, which was open a tiny bit at the top.

"That child should play basketball," said her father, admiring the little girl's aim. As the family lived on the sixth floor of a block of flats, Amy's big brother had to hurry down several flights of stairs to find the little duck out in the car park. After that, Amy's parents kept the bathroom window shut *all* the time.

I'm afraid Amy's next game with the duck was even worse. She (this is quite embarrassing) tried to flush him down the lavatory! Amy was not very pleased when the little duck came bobbing up again, and Amy's mother was not very pleased either at having to fish out the duck and take it away for a thorough cleaning and disinfecting before Amy could have it back again.

Not surprisingly, Amy didn't
want to play with the duck for a
while, but as the years went by, she
found that the little yellow bird was
extremely useful in lots of different
games. It made a wonderful target. As
Amy grew up, the duck had bean
bags, pingpong balls, arrows and
even pretend grenades thrown at it.

Later on, Amy used the duck
for lots of different experiments. She
took it to school and catapulted it

across the playground and into a nearby field to show how levers work. She took it to summer camp and let it float right out into the middle of a lake to practise her life-saving skills. She took it to the park and perched it on the edge of a pond to see how real ducks would

react to it (they either ignored it or pecked it).

After all that, you might have thought that the duck would be rather scratched and bashed, but it actually looked as fresh and bright as the day it was made. With its yellow body and orange beak, the duck looked as good as new.

During all those years, the duck was given many names. Amy's father called it "The Indestructible Duck". Amy's big brother called it "The Unthinkable Unsinkable", but Amy one day named her duck after one of her teachers, who had a voice rather like a quack! After that, it was always Della Duck.

You might think that Della Duck had already had enough adventures to last a liftetime, but Amy had not finished with her yet. In her last year at school, Amy took part in a balloon race. You probably know all about them. Hundreds of people write their names and addresses on labels hanging from balloons. Then the balloons are released and float far away. When the balloons finally come to rest, sometimes months later, anyone who finds them can post off the label, saying where the balloon was found. The person whose balloon is found to have travelled the farthest is the winner.

It would be silly, really, to

attach anything else to the balloon, because it would weigh the balloon down and stop it travelling so far, but one or two members of Amy's class started adding little things to their balloons, and the craze spread. Some people tied on a tiny teddy bear or a photograph of themselves. I don't suppose I need to tell you what Amy decided to tie on to her balloon.

At last the day came when all the balloons were released. Up they went, pink, purple, blue, yellow and green — and one of them had a very brave little duck attached to it!

After a few days, some of the labels from the balloons began to arrive. They had been found many miles away. After a few weeks, even more labels had been returned, and some of them came from hundreds of miles away. But as the weeks turned into months, there was no news of Amy's balloon, or of her old friend Della Duck.

"The balloon might have landed in the middle of a forest or in a desert," said Amy's brother. "No one will ever find it there. Or it might have come down over the sea."

"Well, that would be all right," retorted Amy. "We all know that Della can float. In fact, that duck is impossible to sink."

"True enough," said her brother,

"but that doesn't mean that anyone would *find* her. There's an awful lot of ocean out there, after all."

Even several months after the balloon competition, labels were still arriving, even though the finishing date had passed. A very few balloons had travelled right across the sea and reached other countries. Some of the balloon-senders began writing to the people who had returned the labels, for they felt as if they were special penfriends.

But there was no news of Della. Finally, Amy had to admit that it was very unlikely that the duck would now be found. It could be anywhere in the world by now.

"You're right," Amy told her big brother. "That duck could have fallen in a quarry or a jungle. I just wish I knew where Della was, that's all. I'd just like to *know*."

"Well, you played with that duck longer than I ever thought you would," laughed her brother. "It's the most successful present I've ever given you."

On Amy's next birthday, her brother gave her a tiny box. "I thought we should mark a sad occasion," he smiled. "I hope you like them." Inside the box was a pair of tiny earrings — shaped like ducks!

"Now I'll never forget Della," laughed Amy, "wherever she is!"

It was not long before Amy left school. She had been wondering for a long time what kind of job she might like to do. Somehow, thinking about Della and where she might be in the world made Amy feel that she too would like to travel — not attached to a balloon, perhaps! Amy was lucky to find a job quite soon that was just what she wanted. She worked for a travel agency, and after a year or so began to travel all over the world, seeing many of the places that she had only dreamed of before.

Amy loved her job, especially as she sometimes was able to stay a few extra days in the places she

visited, so that she could have a
little holiday of her own. It was
when she was lying on a beautiful,
sunny beach on the island of
Hawaii that the most extraordinary
thing happened.

Amy was feeling hot and went
down to the edge of the sea for a

cooling swim. But as she came to the edge of the water, Amy kicked something in the sand. She thought it was a shell or a pebble and almost didn't bother to look down, but something made her kneel down on the warm sand and take a look. A little orange beak was poking out of the sand!

"Della!" cried Amy, brushing away the rest of the sand. It certainly was a little yellow duck, and it *looked* just like Della, but whether it really was that famous duck I couldn't say.

Amy wrapped the duck up carefully and sent it to her brother, who now had a little boy of his own. "For Toby," she wrote on the label, "hoping Della has even more adventures with you."

Well, she did, you know, but that is quite another story and for another time…

Princess Dreamy

ONCE UPON A TIME, there was a Princess who spent her life dreaming. Even in the middle of the day, you could find her sitting by herself, fast asleep or simply gazing into space. The King and Queen were rather worried about this, so they called all the most respected doctors in the land to give their considered opinions.

"It is a grave disease," said one doctor, "called *somnomulous revex*. Only very, very intelligent and sensitive people can catch it. Indeed, almost all the cases that have been recorded have been among royalty. Why, the King of Pandango suffered for years."

"And is there a cure?" asked the King, anxiously.

"Alas, Your Majesty, there are some afflictions that nobility must bear," said the first doctor. "I can prescribe some medicines that will ensure your daughter's good health, but I cannot take away her dreamy condition."

The second doctor stepped boldly forward.

"I must disagree with my learned colleague," he said. "The Princess's condition is not caused by an illness at all. She has clearly been bewitched. We shall need to find some powerful magic to counteract the spell that has been cast upon

her. I could recommend someone, if
Your Majesty wishes. I'm afraid that
if an antidote to the spell is not
found, your daughter will stay like
this for ever."

"That's dreadful," said the King.
"Yes, please, do give me the name of
a reliable … er … spellbinder."

But the third doctor was
already bustling forward.

"With all respect to my most
esteemed colleagues," she said, "what
I have heard so far has been
complete nonsense from first to last.
It is quite plain to me that someone
has put a sleeping draught into your
daughter's food. You should inter-
rogate all your servants and have

every morsel of her food checked by a reliable taster. I have the names of several reputable practitioners here if Your Majesty wishes. I can vouch for each and every one of them personally. I think Your Majesty will find that after a few days, the Princess will be her old self again."

"By all means give me the name of a good taster," said the King, although he privately wondered how his daughter was going to be able to eat *anything* if a taster ate every morsel — there wouldn't be any untasted morsels left!

Now a fourth doctor pushed his way to the front.

"We have heard a number of

extraordinary opinions here today," he said, "and I don't doubt that my colleagues have all diagnosed your daughter in good faith, but they could not be more wrong. The Princess has quite obviously been hypnotised. It may have been a person who did it, or the Princess may have inadvertently hypnotised herself by listening too long to the ticking of a clock or the dripping of a tap."

"There are no dripping taps in *my* palace," put in the Queen, rather sharply. "But please do go on, doctor."

The fourth doctor blushed but continued.

"We shall need a very skilled

treatment to bring the Princess back to her old self," he said. "Luckily, I myself trained in Zurich under the great Professor Pamplemouse. I would be willing to undertake the cure at once, but of course I would need all these people to be cleared from the room." With a sweeping gesture of his arm, the doctor indicated all the other doctors and courtiers standing around the King and Queen.

The King looked at his wife a little desperately. Then he turned to the crowd.

"Naturally, the Queen and I are anxious to do whatever is necessary to cure our only child," he said. "We have heard many learned opinions today, and we must think carefully about what to do. I beg you to leave us now and allow us to think over what you have said. We will give our decision in the morning."

The doctors bowed and walked backwards out of the room. Some of them were clearly not used to this manoeuvre, for they fell over their gowns and had to be rescued by the courtiers standing by. It was a sight that would normally have made the King roar with laughter, but today he was much too worried about his daughter to smile.

Soon there was no one in the room but the King, the Queen, the

Princess and the little serving maid who looked after her. The Princess sat dreamily looking out of the castle window, paying no attention at all as the little maid combed her long, dark hair.

The King and Queen sat down together to discuss the opinions of the four doctors and decide what to do about their daughter.

"I don't know about *you*, my dear," said the King, "but I am well and truly confused. Can all these experts be right? Surely our darling girl cannot be so unfortunate as to be suffering from *somno*-something, *and* an evil spell, *and* a sleeping draught, *and* hypnotism all at the same time? That would be dreadful."

"I agree with you," said the Queen. "All of the diagnoses sounded sensible at the time, but now I don't know what to think. I suppose we could try each of the cures in turn?"

"And put our daughter through

four lots of treatment?" asked the King. "That would surely make her worse than she is now. After all, it's not that she is in pain, or even unhappy. She just isn't exactly *with* us most of the time."

"You are right, my dear, of course," said the Queen. "Our daughter's wellbeing must be our first concern. But I am still uncertain about what to do."

Just then, a little voice from the corner of the room spoke up. It was the serving maid.

"Excuse me, Your Majesties," she said timidly, "but I spend a great deal of time with the Princess. Might I just say something myself?"

"Of course you may," said the Queen kindly. "I know that you are very fond of your mistress and would not want any harm to come to her. What is your opinion of what we have heard today?"

"Well, Madam," said the little maid, curtseying deeply, "I have seven older sisters, and I have seen every one of them suffering from much the same illness as the Princess."

The King was a little shocked. "You mean it's not an illness that only royalty can suffer from?" he asked with a frown.

"I don't think so," said the little maid. "I think it is something that

almost anyone can suffer from. My
sisters were just like this. They sat by
themselves. They sighed and didn't
hear people talking to them. They
gazed out of the window all the
time. But I am very happy to say that
each one of them has now
recovered."

"So what was this illness from which they all suffered?" demanded the King, although the Queen was beginning to look as though she understood, and a small smile played about her lips.

Before the little maid could answer, she turned to the King and said, "You know, I had forgotten, but I believe I suffered from much the same malady around the time I first met you, my dear."

The maid smiled too, for the Queen was blushing and looking very pretty.

"Well, you two seem to know what you're talking about," muttered the King, a little gruffly. "Suppose you let a chap who's still in the dark into the secret?"

The little maid curtseyed again. "To put it plainly, Your Majesty," she said. "I believe that the Princess is in love."

"In love?" cried the King. "Why, that's preposterous! She's much too young, and besides, who can she possibly have met that she could be in love with?"

"Don't be so silly, dear. She is two years older than I was when I married you," said the Queen briskly. "And if you remember, young Prince Beaumont was here only last month. He stopped by on his way to visit his aunt, the Grand Duchess."

At the mention of Prince Beaumont's name, the silent Princess turned first white and then pink, causing the Queen and the serving maid to look triumphantly at each other. The King groaned loudly.

"I see only too clearly that I shall have no say in this matter," he said, "although in truth I like young Beaumont well enough, and it could have been much, much worse. If she wants that young Princeling, and he feels the same, I won't stand in their way."

At that, the Princess ran across the room and threw her arms around her father. Having spent several secret afternoons with the

Prince, she knew only too well that he had the same feelings for her as she had for him. The King was astonished, but pleased. And the Queen immediately began to plan the biggest royal wedding that the world had ever seen.

As for the little serving maid, she became a Lady-in-Waiting of the First Rank, for when it comes to knowing what is the matter with ordinary mortals, common sense is often a great deal more useful than any amount of learning, even from Professor Pamplemouse in Zurich!

The House That Slept

NOW EVERYONE knows that human beings are not the only creatures who like to curl up and go to sleep. Cats love to sleep in the sunshine. Ducks tuck their heads under their wings on the pond. And some animals, such as tortoises, sleep for months and months at a time. But did you know that houses sometimes sleep too? This is the story of a house that slept.

There was once a little house at the edge of a wood. It had red tiles on the roof and a green front door. It was a dear little house, and the family that lived in it loved it very much.

There were six of them altogether. Mr and Mrs Ruggles had four children. That was a lot of people to squeeze into a very little house, but they were a happy family and got along very well. Mr Ruggles worked in the woodland, clearing fallen branches and felling trees when the time was right. He walked to his work each day and enjoyed it enormously. He felt that he was a lucky man to live where he wanted to live and work where he wanted to work.

Mrs Ruggles worked in the nearby town. She was a nurse, visiting people in their homes and making sure that they were taking care of themselves properly. She too enjoyed her work. She even enjoyed the journey into town each day, driving along the pretty, winding road through the beautiful countryside.

The children went to school in the town too, but they were always glad to come home to their little house next to the wood.

The family took care of each other, and they took care of the little house, too. Each year, Mr Ruggles climbed up on to the roof (while Mrs Ruggles stood below and called to him to be careful) and checked that none of the red tiles were loose or broken. And every other year, Mr and Mrs Ruggles painted the front door and the windows, to keep out the rain and frost. As they grew older, the children helped with the painting, too, so that a job that once took a whole week was finished in two days.

The children grew up, as children do, and one by one they left home to study, or work, or find homes of their own.

Soon, only Mr and Mrs Ruggles were left. At first the house seemed very big without the children, but Mrs Ruggles said that they couldn't possibly go and live somewhere smaller because the children would need somewhere to sleep when they came home for visits. Mr Ruggles was secretly very relieved to hear his wife say this. He loved living so near the forest, and he loved the old house. It had so many happy memories.

But time passed, and first Mr

Ruggles and then Mrs Ruggles retired from their work. They still loved their home, so they decided not to move, although their children all thought that would be a good idea.

"It's so lonely out here," they said. "What if one of you became ill and needed a doctor?"

Mr and Mrs Ruggles laughed.

"We're not quite in our dotage yet, you know!" they said.

But it was harder now to look after the little house, even without having to worry about work as well. Now that there were only the two of them to do the painting, it took three weeks – much longer than before. And they had to call a man out from the nearby town to check the tiles, because Mrs Ruggles said that it just wasn't safe for her husband to climb on to the roof any more.

There were other problems, too. Although he still liked to live near the wood and watch as it changed through the seasons, Mr Ruggles was upset by the way his old work was now done by machines and lads who had no feeling for the beautiful trees.

"It's not the same," he said. "It breaks my heart to see them carting logs away as if they were sacks of coal. Those trees are living things.

They should be treated with respect."

Then, one very cold winter, snow lay so thickly around the little house that Mr and Mrs Ruggles were trapped for two weeks. They were no longer strong enough to clear the snow from the driveway, and they were worried about dangerous ice on the winding road into town.

The couple sat in their armchairs either side of the fire and looked at each other.

"We've had a wonderful time in this old house," said Mr Ruggles, "but it's time we moved into a little bungalow in town."

"Yes," said Mrs Ruggles. "I shall

be sad to leave here, but it will be a relief, too, in a way."

So Mr and Mrs Ruggles locked the green front door for the last time and followed the van containing their furniture and all their possessions along the winding road. They were very happy in their new home and soon hardly ever thought of the little house near the wood.

Meanwhile, a board was put up outside the house. "To Let," it said. "Contact Buttle and Bung, Estate Agents." Several people came to look at the house, but it was either too small, or too far from town, or too lonely, or too old-fashioned. After a few months, the estate agents' board fell down in a high wind, and no one bothered to put it up again. Standing by itself, next to the lovely woodland, the house fell fast asleep.

Of course, it didn't shut its eyes, for houses don't have eyes, but they have windows, and these gradually grew dull and dusty. The paint on the front door began to fade and peel. The red tiles, which Mr Ruggles had looked after so carefully, began to slip and slide, and some of them fell off altogether.

Then, of course, the rain began to trickle into the house. It dripped through the ceilings and made puddles on the floors.

But the house wasn't empty. Oh

no. All kinds of little creatures made their home there. Spiders filled the corners with cobwebs. Little ants and beetles crept along the dusty floorboards. Moths fluttered around the windows. In the walls, little feet could be heard scampering night and day, as a group of mice moved in and brought up their own families. An owl perched on the guttering some moonlit nights.

So the house slept on, and the trees crept nearer to it, until their

branches touched the roof and pushed more of the tiles into the garden. Well, it wasn't a garden any more, really. The plants rampaged everywhere, and some of them reached right up to the bedroom windows. If you weren't looking carefully, you could walk right past the house and not know it was there. It was having a long, long sleep.

Then, one day, Mr and Mrs Ruggles' eldest son came back to visit the place where he had grown up. He brought his wife and their two young children with him.

"I'm so looking forward to seeing it," said the younger Mrs

Ruggles. "You've talked so much about it. I'm sure it was a perfect place for a child to live."

When he turned off the long, winding road from town, her husband couldn't believe his eyes. The trees and hedges along the drive had grown so much.

"It all looks so different," he said. "And, oh no, I don't believe it! The house has gone!"

"No," said his wife, for she had seen a chimney sticking up above the bushes. "It's still here, hidden behind all this greenery."

"It's a secret house," laughed the children. "Let's go and look inside! It's an adventure!"

It took ages to push aside the branches and wade through the grass to the front door. The lock had rotted away, so it was easy to swing the door back on its creaking hinges and step inside.

"Be careful," warned Mr Ruggles. "The floorboards may have rotted,

and it doesn't look as if the ceiling is too safe either."

The grown-ups and the children tiptoed through the rooms. The house was in a terrible state, but somehow it still felt like a happy place to be.

As the children ran out to explore the garden — which they called "the jungle" — their mother and father looked at each other and saw that they were both thinking the same thing.

Mrs Ruggles laughed. "It would be mad!" she said. "There's so much work to do on it!"

Mr Ruggles smiled too. "It would be stupid," he agreed.

His wife sighed. "It would be a wonderful place for the children to grow up," she said.

"We'd never find another house in such a beautiful spot," said her husband.

Soon they were both giggling like children.

"It's time we did something completely crazy again," said Mr Ruggles. "Let's go and explore the jungle."

Over the next few weeks, there was more activity around the house than there had been for the last ten years. Trees were cut down, and bushes were pruned. Soon it was possible to reach the front door without a struggle. But still the house slept.

Over the next few months, workmen hammered and sawed. Timbers were renewed and floor-boards replaced. New red tiles were put on the roof, and the front door was mended and painted — green, of course. But still the house slept.

At last the day came when Mr and Mrs Ruggles and their two children moved in. Lights winked at the windows, and the house felt a warmth inside that had been missing for a long time. The house stretched and creaked for a moment — and woke up at last.

The
Day the
Sun Was
Silly

MOST PEOPLE are awake in the daytime and asleep at night. Well, that doesn't always work for babies! And there are people who have to work at night as well. But on the whole, we get up when the sun gets up and go to bed when the sun goes to bed.

Of course, the sun doesn't really go to bed. It just shines on another part of the world. It is always daytime somewhere in the world. And it is always night somewhere else, as well. It works very well. We all get a share of the sun for part of the day.

But long, long ago, there was a day when the sun was very silly. All

day long, he had been shining down
on a beautiful garden. There were
flowers and trees, grass and fountains. It was lovely. The flowers lifted
their pretty faces to say hello to the
sun, and the tiny drops of water that
jumped from the fountains sparkled
like little jewels in the sunlight. The
sun had never seen a more perfect
sight.

"What a shame it will be night time soon," said the sun, "and I will not be able to shine on this garden any more. It's all very annoying. After all, I'm much bigger than anything else in the sky. I should be able to decide what I can do. No one's powerful enough to argue with me!"

So the silly sun carried on shining on the beautiful garden. The flowers stayed open, and the birds carried on singing.

But the garden wasn't meant to have sunshine all the time. Soon the flowers began to droop in the hot sun. The birds began to get hoarse from singing for so long.

The sun was stubborn. He
wanted to prove that he could do
anything he liked.

He was determined to carry on
shining whatever happened.

Of course, the garden wasn't the
only place that was in trouble. All
over the world people were feeling
very confused.

Streetlights came on and looked
quite out of place in the bright
sunshine. Animals that like to come
out at night, such as owls, didn't
know what to do. They were hungry,
but it was much too bright to fly out
of their nests.

In other parts of the world,
there was the opposite problem. It

was still dark, long after it should
have been daytime. Some people
were still in bed, asleep. Others tried
to carry on as usual, eating their
breakfast in the dark and setting off
for work or school with torches. It
was quite hopeless. And all because
the silly sun thought he could do
whatever he liked.

Meanwhile, the moon was
getting very cross. If the sun kept
shining, she couldn't be seen at all.
The stars were invisible too.

Across the huge distances of
space, the moon called out to the
silly old sun.

"Hey! What do you think you're
doing? Everything is dreadful on

earth because you're not doing as you should. We all look up to you, you know."

When he heard that, the sun felt ashamed. He looked down on the beautiful garden and saw that the flowers were drooping and the birds were dropping off their perches with tiredness.

"They all rely on me," he thought. "I must be a sensible old sun in future."

And you know, from that day to this, he has never been silly again. Thank goodness!

The Ship of Dreams

ONCE THERE WAS a mighty ship, with sails of silver and ropes, which are called sheets on a ship, of gold. It had a poop deck and a quarter deck and all the other decks a ship should have. It had portholes and a rudder and masts. But the strange thing is that it didn't have a crew. No, the ship sailed all by itself.

Which ocean did this ship sail upon? Did it cross the great Pacific Ocean or drift across the warm waters of the Indian Ocean? Or did it brave the great storms of the Southern Ocean? No, it sailed none of these great seas. It sailed the skies. For it was a ship of dreams.

If you go sailing on the ship of dreams, you will visit strange lands and meet people who look almost familiar. You might zoom through the skies or plunge to the bottom of the seas. You could ride on the back of a tiger or take tea with a flea. The ship of dreams can sail anywhere, but it always comes back to port in the morning.

Once there was a little boy who wanted more than anything else to go sailing on the ship of dreams. But in the morning, he could never remember if he had dreamed or not. At school, his friends would talk about the wonderful dreams they had had, but poor Peter could

never remember a single one. After a while, he felt so left out that I'm afraid he began to invent dreams that he had not had at all.

"Last night," he would boast, "I dreamed I was riding on a camel. It had a bridle of gold and reins of silver. We travelled over the desert for miles and miles, until we came to a beautiful palace. Everyone bowed down when I went into it. I was the Prince of the whole country, and I owned the palace and everything in it."

"Wow!" said the other children. "I wish we had dreams like that."

"Oh, that was nothing," said Peter. "The night before that I

dreamed I was diving in the ocean
and saw a wreck on the sea bed. I
swam down to it and found a casket
full of jewels. They glinted and
glittered in the blue water. But just
as I was swimming down to reach
them, a huge shark came charging
towards me. It opened its mouth
and…"

"Yes, yes?" cried the children.

"…and I woke up," said Peter.

Peter soon found that everyone
wanted to hear about his fabulous
dreams. He began to make them
more and more elaborate and
extraordinary. One day, as he was
telling the children about a trip
through a forest, where wolves were

howling, his teacher happened to overhear him.

"With an imagination like that, Peter," she said, "you should be a writer. You have kept your friends spellbound for an hour."

And when Peter grew up, he did become a writer, a very famous writer. His stories were read and loved the world over.

When Peter was an old, old man, a journalist came to see him to write a story about his life.

"How lucky you were to have such rich dreams to draw on in your early years," he said.

"No," said Peter. "In fact, I did not have dreams at all, but that was lucky too, in a way. I had to use my imagination to make up strange tales for myself, because as far as I know, I never dreamed."

"But everyone dreams!" the young man protested. "It must just be that you don't remember."

"I don't know," said Peter. "I only know that as far as I'm concerned, the ship of dreams has never stopped for me, and I would give all the stories I have ever written and all the money I have ever made for one trip upon that wonderful ship."

The journalist left the old man sitting looking wistfully out to sea. He wished that it was in his power to give the great author what he wished for.

But that very night, Peter dreamed of a fabulous ship, with sails of silver and sheets of gold. It was the ship of dreams, and he ran on board as nimbly as he would have done when he was a boy. The places Peter visited that night and the

people he met will remain a secret for ever, for his first and last great dream was one from which he did not awake. He has sailed on for ever, into the setting sun.

The King of the Forest

ONCE UPON A TIME, there was a King who loved trees. Ever since he was a baby Princeling, when his nurse put him out in his crib to look up at the green leaves of a mighty oak waving above him, he had loved all living things. But trees made his heart sing and his eyes grow misty. He thought they were the most beautiful things in the world.

When he was a boy, the King climbed every tree he could find. From high in the branches, he could almost feel that he was part of the tree, swaying in the wind, warm in the summer sunshine. He wished that he could live there for ever, and often spent the night in a little treehouse built for him by the Royal Carpenter. There he could forget he was a Prince and pretend to be like other children. For Princes are brought up to know that they will one day have the terrible responsibility of being King. Some Princes cannot wait to sit upon the throne,

but others long for a quiet life, doing the things they love.

The hero of this story was just like that. If he had had his way, he would have stayed all day among his beloved trees, far away from the busy world of life at court.

However, the day came, as everyone expected, when the old King died. The new King wept for his father and for himself, for he felt that his freedom was over.

No longer could the new King wander in the woods he loved. He had to sit in his palace, reading documents and listening to the requests of his subjects.

Not all of the work was

boring. The King enjoyed helping people who needed his aid, and some of the pageants and processions were very impressive, but he had no time to walk beneath the shady boughs or tend the oak trees around the palace.

One day, however, as he looked at an ancient map of his kingdom, he noticed a large area of green at the very edge of his realm.

"What is that?" he asked his Chief Minister.

"That, Sire, is an ancient wood, planted by your great-great-great-great-great-great-great-great grandfather. Most of it has been cut down now, which is why you do not see it on more modern maps of our beloved country."

"So when you say my great-great-whatever planted it...," the King began.

"Of course, Sire, I mean that he instructed that it should be planted. He didn't go out there himself. Ha ha! No, no, royal workers planted the trees under royal instructions." The King felt happier than he had at any time since he came to the throne.

"This," he said, "is a custom that I feel is worth reviving. We shall plant a new royal forest, and it will bigger and better than any forest ever planted."

Despite his busy workload, over the next few months, the King somehow managed to find time to supervise every detail of the plans for the new forest. It was going to be magnificent.

"I should like planting to begin immediately," he said, when the site had been chosen. "Send the Chief Forester to me."

But the Chief Forester looked very worried when the King outlined his plans.

"I don't think that will be possible, Sire," he said.

"Not possible?" cried the King. "Why ever not? We have the men. We have the land."

"But we don't have the plants, Sire," said the Chief Forester. "We will need thousands and thousands, no, probably millions and millions of little oak tree plants, and there are not that number to be had in this kingdom or the next. Indeed, I am sure that there are not so many baby trees of the right kind to be found in the whole world."

The King paused. There was no doubt in his mind that his Chief Forester was absolutely right. Why had he not thought of it before? Would his great plan have to be abandoned after all?

"Let me think about it," said the King, "and come to see me at the same time tomorrow. This will be an extraordinary forest. We shall need an extraordinary plan."

All night long, the King tossed and turned. He was determined that his forest would be planted.

"I need this forest," he muttered to himself. "The people need this forest. The King's forest. The people's forest. *The people's forest!*" That was it! The King fell into a deep and peaceful sleep.

Next morning, the King could hardly wait for his Chief Forester to arrive. When he did, the King explained his plan. The Forester's eyes widened, but he was smiling. It would work!

Losing no time, the King called for a proclamation to be sent to every part of his realm.

ALL SUBJECTS

are invited to

PLANT AN ACORN

for the Royal Forest

Full instructions given.

Your tree could live for a thousand years!

It was a wonderful idea. There was hardly a person in the kingdom who didn't plant a little acorn in a pot, or a jar, or a cup. Tiny children of two years old planted them. Venerable old gentlemen of ninety-two planted them. All anybody could talk about, wherever you went, was how well their acorns were growing. The newspapers gave advice on the best growing conditions. Magazines devoted whole articles to the best way to talk to your acorn, for one of the greatest gardeners in the land had announced that all plants do better if they are talked to regularly. Another magazine suggested songs that could be sung to the acorns, while yet another actually asked a composer to write a special acorn song.

Soon, little shoots began to appear, then two little leaves. After two years, sturdy little oak tree plants stood on the doorstep of every house in the land.

At last, the Great Planting could begin.

It took five hundred men a whole year to plant the forest. After that, a hundred men tended the small plants and watched them grow into slender saplings.

Well, that was long ago, but the forest still stands. Now, not only the King but all his people can walk proudly under the majestic trees and say to their children, "Your great-great-great-great grandfather (or grandmother!) planted one of these trees."

The people love the forest almost as much as the King who planted it. Although he died long ago, he is remembered by everyone in the country as the King of the Forest. If he is looking down on it now, he will be weeping for joy — or making plans for another forest of his beloved oak trees!

Bubbles
at
Bathtime

ONCE UPON A TIME, there was a little boy who really hated his bathtime. He would yell and scream and kick his feet. It was terrible. And the funny thing is that there wasn't anything about his bath itself that he didn't like.

Here is what had happened. When Robert was a little tiny boy, he enjoyed being up and about so much that he never wanted to go to bed. He soon learned that bathtime meant bedtime would soon follow, so he started protesting as soon as his mummy began to run the water. It was dreadful. The yelling and screaming and kicking were so horrible that his poor mother dreaded bathtime more than cleaning the oven or opening the electricity bill.

The silly thing is that the yelling and screaming and kicking made Robert so tired that he always fell asleep the moment his mummy popped him into his little bed. So nobody realised that it was really bed-time and not bathtime he didn't like.

Sometimes we carry on doing things even when we can't remember why we do them any more. They become a habit. Bathtimes were like that for Robert. Although he was quite a big boy now, nearly old enough to go to school, he still made a dreadful fuss at bathtime.

One morning, Robert received a

surprise parcel. It wasn't his birthday or anything like that, so he couldn't wait to open it. Mummy looked at the writing and said she thought it was from Aunty Sue.

Robert liked Aunty Sue. She always sent him presents that were just right. He tore off the outer wrapping. Inside the brown paper was another parcel, wrapped in coloured paper. This one had a strange label:

> ## My name is
> ## Bubbles

Whatever did *that* mean? As he ripped away the wrapping paper, Robert's face fell. Inside was a toy duck, the kind you have in the bath. It was quite a nice duck, certainly, with a yellow body and an orange beak, but still it was babyish, he thought. And anyway, it reminded him of that word beginning with *b*!

Robert pushed the duck across the table in disgust and hurried off.

That night, as Robert kicked and screamed in his bath, he noticed that his mother had put the duck on the shelf near the taps. Remembering his awful disappointment earlier in the day made Robert yell even more.

Just when Robert's poor mother

was thinking that she couldn't stand *any* more, the telephone rang. The telephone was out on the landing, so the poor woman quickly went to answer it, leaving the bathroom door open so that she could see her son and make sure he was all right.

"Hello?" said Robert's mummy.

"Hello!" said Bubbles the duck.

What? Robert stopped his screaming for a moment in surprise. He thought for a moment that the duck had spoken, but of course that was silly.

"Hello," said Bubbles again. "It's Robert, isn't it?"

"Yes," said Robert, before he'd had time to think.

"Well, what's the trouble?" asked the duck in a friendly way.

"The trouble?" asked Robert, still not able to believe his ears.

"Yes. I couldn't help noticing that you were making quite a noise just now. Is something the matter?"

Robert shook his head like a puppy dog. He thought he might have water in his ears. There must be some reason why he kept thinking the duck was speaking. And here it was doing it again!

"Well?" the duck persisted. "Is something wrong?"

"No," said Robert. "Yes, no!"

"You don't seem to be able to make up your mind," commented

Bubbles. "Is the bath too hot or cold for you?"

"No," said Robert, rubbing his eyes in disbelief.

"Are you afraid of water?"

"No," said the little boy again.

"Well, is it soap you don't like?"

"No, soap is all right," said Robert, frowning.

"I'm sorry," said the duck. "I simply don't understand. Why were you screaming and yelling if you don't mind having a bath?"

Robert looked down. He felt rather silly.

"I don't know," he said.

"You don't know? A big boy like you? Well, that is very strange. I must say that in all my years of being in baths, I've never seen anything like it."

"Haven't you?" asked Robert, feeling very small.

"Certainly not," said the duck firmly. "Now is this kind of thing going to continue? Because I'm not sure I can live next to a bath that has

such a noisy boy in it."

Robert thought for a minute. "I don't think I'm going to do it any more," he said, to his surprise.

"Good," said Bubbles. "Then I'll be happy to stay and we'll be the best of friends."

Later that week, Robert heard his mother talking to a friend.

"You know," she said, "all these years of screaming and all he wanted was for me not to be in the room. After all, he's nearly old enough to go to school. Why ever didn't I think of it before?"

Well, I'm not going to tell her what really happened. Are you?

The Last Tree

ONCE UPON A TIME, there was an island covered with trees. They grew so thickly that their branches met overhead. No light from the sun could filter down to the forest floor, so nothing grew there. And as nothing grew except trees, there was also nothing for most small animals and insects to eat. Only a few creatures survived in the topmost branches of the trees, where the sunlight dappled the glossy green leaves.

One day, a scientist came to the island. He examined the trees and the living things that shared the island with them. Then he sent in his report to the ruler of the country that owned the island. He reported that trees had overrun the island, destroying other plant life and restricting the wildlife that could survive there. He advised that exactly half of the trees should be cut down to allow light to reach the forest floor and then other species would begin to thrive again on the island.

The ruler to whom the report was sent hesitated. He formed several committees to discuss the matter. He asked another scientist to prepare his own report, to check the findings of the first scientist.

At last, the ruler found that the advice he was receiving. He ordered that half the trees on the island should be cut down.

It took a long while for the work to be carried out. There was nowhere on the island that the woodcutters to stay, so they had to travel to the island each day by boat. They had only a few hours to work before the boat returned to take them back home to the mainland before nightfall.

When the woodcutters had finished their work, all the fallen trees had to be removed. Again committees, special enquiries and two scientists suggested suitable methods. In the end, it was a small boy, who had been reading his sister's encyclopedia, who offered the solution. The trees were pushed into the sea and floated on the tide to the mainland.

No one visited the island. The plan was to leave it undisturbed to see what new kinds of plants and

animals would begin to live there.
After seven years, the original scientist
returned to the island.

It was a terrible disappointment.
Instead of leaving space for new
plants to grow, the felling of the trees
had given the remaining trees extra
space to grow taller themselves. Their
branches grew longer, until they
touched each other overhead. Just as
before, not a single ray of sunlight
reached the forest floor. Only the
creatures that had survived before the
trees were cut down still lived on the
island, high in the branches.

The ruler demanded that new
studies and new committees should
be set up. Another plan was needed
for the island. It didn't seem to occur

to anyone that the island could simply be left alone.

This time, the advice was more sweeping. All the trees must be cut down to enable other living things to grow on the island and eventually the plan was carried out. Once again, it was a mammoth task. In fact, this time, the trees were bigger and more difficult to fell. When every tree was cut down, they were floated away to the nearby mainland as before.

Another seven years passed before a study was carried out. This time, two scientists visited the island together. As they approached it in their boat, they peered at the horizon, looking for signs of life — a fuzz of green over the island, perhaps, or the beating of wings as a flock of birds rose up at their approach. But they found nothing.

That's right. There were no trees. No birds. No insects. No plants. No animals. There were no living things on the island at all. It was dead.

The scientists spent two days searching for even the tiniest sign of life. Finally, they were forced to admit that even seaweed did not grow on the rocks around the shore.

Something had plainly gone wrong. The ruler set up a committee as usual, to find out where mistakes had been made. On the last day of the enquiry, a very important witness came to give his opinion.

This old man was well known as

a world authority on islands and the living things that make their homes on them. He was rather frail now, but his mind was as sharp as ever. Everyone waited with interest for his views.

"Is it true," he was asked, "that there is nothing living on the island?"

"Yes, that is true," he replied.

"And is it a fact that there are no living things *able* to survive on the island?"

"No," he said, "that is not so."

"So what are these creatures or plants that could do well on so barren a piece of ground?"

The old man looked around at everyone in the room.

Why, trees," he said.